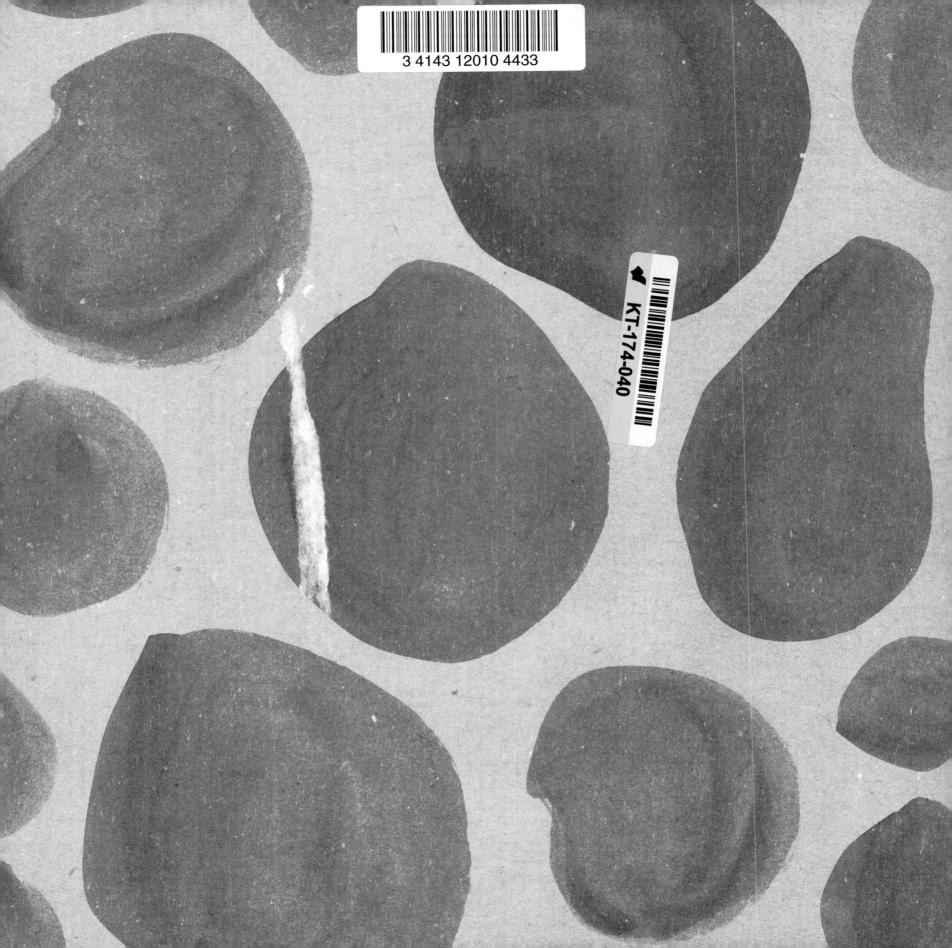

To Helen and Gabby - MR

For my parents and the art den under the stairs
where it all began - CP

SIMON & SCHUSTER
First published in Great Britain in 2017 by Simon & Schuster UK Ltd
1st Floor, 222 Gray's Inn Road, London WC1X 8HB
A CBS Company

Text copyright © 2017 Michelle Robinson
Illustrations copyright © 2017 Claire Powell

ISBN: 978-0-8570-7598-7 (HB) • ISBN: 978-0-8570-7599-4 (PB) • ISBN: 978-1-4711-6335-7 (eBook)
Printed in China • 1 2 3 4 5 6 7 8 9 10

HAVe You SEEn My GiRaffe?

michelle RoBinson & ClaiRe Powell

SIMON & SCHUSTER
London   New York   Sydney   Toronto   New Delhi

They used to give away goldfish at the fairground.

Not any more.

These days you're more likely to win a giraffe.

I know what you're thinking.
Cute pet.

But I bet your parents won't think so.

'Sure, he's cute,' they'll say,
'but he's also BIG and clumsy.

And besides,

there's nowhere to keep him.'

But what do they know?

He could fit in there.

Squish in here.

Or squeeeeeze in there.

Okay, maybe not.

'He's **NOT** staying here!'

That's what they think.

Your giraffe can stay –

he just needs a very good hiding place.

Let's think. Where's the best place to hide a giraffe?

A forest, you say? Good idea!

A forest is just the sort of place for a BIG, clumsy animal to hide.

But forests take a long time to grow ...

So, while you're waiting, make your giraffe a temporary disguise.

He could be a very spotty lamp.

A very weird dog.

Or a very tall friend.

If all else fails, you can always camouflage him.

Either paint your whole house like a giraffe . . .

. . . or paint your whole giraffe like a house.

Oops.

Hmmm, maybe your parents were right after all.

He is big.

And clumsy.

And there really isn't **anywhere** to keep him.

JEEPERS!

And **now** there's nowhere to keep us, either!

Jeepers? That would have been a great name!

But that doesn't matter now –

you can't keep him.

You'll just have to take him back
where he came from . . .

...THE FOREST?!

You were right all along.

This is just the place to keep
a big, clumsy animal,
(called Jeepers).

Now your giraffe will **NEVER** have to hide, ever again.

Unless, of course . . .

. . . he wants to!